# MARTHA SPEAKS™

# Toy Trouble

DISCARDED

Adaptation by Karen Barss

Based on a TV series teleplay written by Raye Lankford

**Based on the characters created by Susan Meddaugh**

HOUGHTON MIFFLIN HARCOURT
Boston • New York • 2010

For information about permission to reproduce selections from this book, write to Permissions, Houghton Mifflin Harcourt Publishing Company, 215 Park Avenue South, New York, New York 10003.

Green Light Readers and its logo are trademarks of Houghton Mifflin Harcourt Publishing Company.

Library of Congress Cataloging-in-Publication Data is on file.

ISBN 978-0-547-21078-0

Design by Bill Smith Group
www.hmhbooks.com
www.marthathetalkingdog.com

Manufactured in China / LEO 10 9 8 7 6 5 4 3 2 1
4500202448

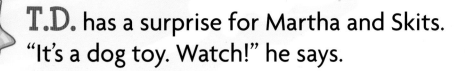

T.D. has a surprise for Martha and Skits.
"It's a dog toy. Watch!" he says.

T.D. puts his fingers into the toy squirrel's front feet.

"Now I pull," he explains, "and let go!"

The toy flies into the air.
It makes a funny noise.
*Chitter-chitter-chitter!*
Martha and Skits run after the toy.

"Skits! Give it!" Martha yells.
Skits growls.
He shakes his head.
"Skits is hogging the toy!" Martha whines.

Helen frowns.
"You have to share."

"T.D. wanted us both to have fun," Martha says. Skits drops the toy.

Martha grins and grabs it.
"Ha-ha! All mine," she says.
Skits barks. *Woof, woof!*
Martha and Skits tug on the toy.

Helen grabs the toy and walks into
the house.
The dogs follow her.
"Why did you take it away?" Martha asks.

"It will stay inside," Helen replies,
"until you learn to play nice."
"That could take forever!" Martha exclaims.

"Come with me," Helen says.
She plays a video on TV.
It is a video about sharing.

Two puppets both want a ball.

A clown sings,
"When there is more than one,
playing is more fun when you share . . ."

"What do you say now?" Helen asks.
Martha turns to Skits.
"Let's call a truce," Martha says.
"No more fighting."

But Martha does not want to share.
She wants to trade toys for the squirrel.
*Woof,* says Skits, shaking his head.
He does not want Martha's toys.

Martha decides to play a trick on Skits.
She points behind Skits with her nose.
"What if I give you *that?*"

When Skits turns away to look,
Martha grabs the squirrel.
Skits chases her, barking.
*Woof! Woof!*

"I told you to share!" Helen says.
Martha laughs. "We *are* sharing."
"How?" Helen asks.

"I made up a new game,"
says Martha.
"I call it Steal the Squirrel."

Martha runs outside.
Skits runs after her.
He grabs the toy and tugs.
*Chitter-chitter-chitter.*

"But you are tugging, not sharing," Helen says.

"This is how dogs play," Martha explains.

"There is still one problem," Helen says.
"I want to play, too!"
"That's the best idea I've heard all day!" Martha says.